This book belongs to:

The Best Ever Ring Bearer

All the Best Things About Being in a Wedding

Illustrated by
Linda Hill Griffith

 sourcebooks

Published by Sourcebooks, Inc.
P.O. Box 4410, Naperville, Illinois 60567-4410
(630) 961-3900
Fax: (630) 961-2168
www.sourcebooks.com

Source of Production: Oceanic Graphic Printing, China
Date of Production: October 2019
Run Number: 5016659

Printed and bound in China.
OGP 20

To My Best Ever
Ring Bearer

David knew something exciting was happening. Uncle Andrew and his girlfriend Sarah were talking to Mommy and Daddy. Everyone was hugging and smiling.

David peeked into the room.

"Come in, David," said Uncle Andrew. "We have some big news!"

"We're going to the zoo?" David *loved* animals.

"Better than that," said Uncle Andrew. "Sarah and I are getting married…and we want you to be the ring bearer!"

"Hooray!" David shouted. "I'm going to be the ring bearer!"

"Uncle Andrew," David said, a little bit nervous, "I'm not sure I'm big enough to be a bear, but I'll try."

Uncle Andrew explained. "Being a ring bearer means that you will be my special helper during our wedding ceremony. You will get to wear a grown-up suit and walk down the aisle holding our rings. It will be very exciting."

David wasn't sure it would be as much fun as the zoo, but he trusted Uncle Andrew.

Daddy and Uncle Andrew took David shopping for clothes to wear to the wedding.

Together they chose a special suit called a tuxedo that matched what the grown-ups would be wearing. David had never worn a grown-up suit before!

David could hardly believe his eyes. "I look just like you, Daddy!"
"You sure do, Son—only far more handsome," Daddy said.

David started to get very excited about being the ring bearer.

"Will I carry the rings in my pocket, Daddy?" he asked.

"No," Daddy explained. "They will be tied to a pillow you'll carry as you walk down the aisle."

The night before the wedding, everyone gathered at the church for a rehearsal.

"When you get to the end of the aisle," Daddy said, "give the pillow and the rings to the best man, Michael."

David smiled. This wasn't very hard at all!

After the rehearsal, everybody in the wedding party had dinner together at a fancy restaurant. Sarah's niece Sophie was there, too. She was going to be the flower girl, another big job.

"You and Sophie must remember to always be polite and patient and calm," Daddy said.

"Okay," Sophie said. "I'll be super-duper good!"

"Me too," David said. "No yelling, no screaming, and no playing in the mud, right?"

Daddy laughed. "That's exactly right!"

David woke up early the day of the wedding and jumped out of bed as fast as he could. He brushed his teeth and washed his face, and he even combed his hair. He was so glad that the big day was finally here.

Daddy helped David get dressed
in his tuxedo and tie his shiny shoes.

"Hurry up," David said. "We don't
want to be late for the wedding!"

"Sarah and Andrew want to have lots of photos to remember their wedding day," Daddy said as they all posed for pictures before the ceremony.

David spotted a small pond with lots of frogs hopping around. One of the frogs—a big one!—hopped toward Sophie's basket, but then David heard Daddy say it was time to walk down the aisle.

All of a sudden, David heard Sarah shouting!

"Somebody do something!" Sarah cried. "There's a frog in the church and he's starting to jump down the aisle!"

David *loved* animals! He could help!

"I'll be right back!" David said, and then as fast as he could, he scooped up that big green frog.

David ran back to the pond and placed the frog into the water.

"Ribbit!" said the frog.

"You're welcome," said David. "But I have to go now. It's time for the wedding!"

"We're so proud of you, David," Daddy said. "You saved the wedding! Now hurry— they're waiting for you to start."

When it was David's turn, he took a deep breath and began to walk down the aisle, slowly and carefully, just like they practiced. Everyone smiled at him.

David felt very proud when Sarah and Uncle Andrew exchanged the rings—he knew they couldn't have done it without him.

After the ceremony, it was time for the wedding reception—a big fun party to celebrate the wedding.

The bride and groom danced together, and then it was time to eat. David's favorite part of the night was the wedding cake…it was almost bigger than he was!

David hardly felt tired at all. He couldn't believe it was almost time to go home.

Uncle Andrew came over and shook David's hand.

"Thank you for being my special helper, David. And thanks for taking care of that frog. You are the best ever ring bearer!"

"I had fun," David said. "But next time, do you think we could go to the zoo instead?"